Little Pierre

A Cajun Story from Louisiana

ROBERT D. SAN SOUCI   Illustrated by **DAVID CATROW**

24636329

Silver Whistle
HARCOURT, INC.
Orlando   Austin   New York   San Diego   Toronto   London

Cajun [cay-jun]	French-speaking people who live in the Louisiana Bayou country; descendants of Acadian exiles forced out of Nova Scotia by the English in 1755
Lousianne [lou-zee-ann]	Louisiana
maman [mah-mahn]	mama (French)
papa [pah-pah]	daddy (French)
Pierre [pee-yair]	stone (equivalent of Peter)
Pierrette [pee-yair-et]	small stone (feminine or diminutive of Pierre)
Poo-yi! [pooh-yee]	Ugh! Phew! (expression of disgust)
rou garou [rooh garoo]	werewolf (from French, *loup garou*)
Ti-Poucet [tee-poo-say]	Little Tom Thumb (Poucet means Tom Thumb; the use of Ti—"little"—is from the French *petit* and emphasizes his smallness.)
très jolie [tray zho-lee]	very pretty (French)

Text copyright © 2003 by Robert D. San Souci / Illustrations copyright © 2003 by David Catrow

Library of Congress Cataloging-in-Publication Data
San Souci, Robert D.
Little Pierre: a Cajun story from Louisiana/by Robert D. San Souci; illustrated by David Catrow.
p. cm. "Silver Whistle."
"The adventures of Little Pierre are based on the stories of Poucet or Ti-Poucet (Little Tom Thumb, Thumbling)"—Author's note.
Summary: A very tiny but clever boy outwits his older brothers, an ogre, an alligator, and a giant catfish to rescue a rich man's daughter in this Cajun version of a French fairy tale.
[1. Fairy tales. 2. Folklore—France] I. Perrault, Charles, 1628—1703. Petit Poucet. II. Catrow, David, ill. III. Title.
PZ8.S248Lk 2003   398.2'0944'01—dc21   [E]   2002152700
ISBN 0-15-202482-4

First edition
H G F E D C B A

Manufactured in China

The illustrations in this book were done in watercolor on bristol board.
The display type was hand-lettered by Judythe Sieck.
The text type was set in Goudy Village.
Color separations by Bright Arts Ltd., Hong Kong
Manufactured by South China Printing Company, Ltd., China
This book was printed on totally chlorine-free Enso Stora Matte paper.
Production supervision by Sandra Grebenar and Ginger Boyer
Designed by Judythe Sieck

For Dirk, with thanks for years of friendship, support, and making sure
the rit-ma-tick in my office always adds up
—R. S. S.

For Deborah,
I tink it is—isn't it?
—D. C.

In the old days, ogres, gators, and *rou garous*—werewolves—haunted the bayous of Lousianne. Back then a trapper, Pierre, and his old woman, Pierrette, raised four boys. They called their sons Big Pierre; Fat Pierre; Wise Pierre, who knew arithmetic; and Foolish Pierre, whose brain always hurt when he tried to think.

When another brother came along, Pierre said, "He so small-small, I gonna call him Little Pierre."

Little Pierre had more brains than all of his brothers put together. His *maman* and *papa* loved him, their last child. They called him heaven's little gift.

His brothers called him runt. They didn't like Little Pierre, because he worked hard from the time he could wash a dish or lift a hoe. The others were so lazy, they ate breakfast, dinner, and supper in the morning. This saved the trouble of sitting down and getting up more than once. Then they said, "It ain't proper to work after supper," and sat in rockers on the porch all day.

Little Pierre helped his *papa* catch catfish or trap muskrat, which is the only way the family got by.

One day word came that Marie-Louise, the daughter of the richest man around, had been stolen by the ogre who lived deep in the cypress swamp. Her *papa* offered a big reward and Marie-Louise's hand in marriage to anyone who rescued her.

"We can get that girl and money, us," said Big Pierre. "Then we each wouldn't have to work no more."

"We don't work now," said Fat Pierre. "Seem a lotta trouble to not get what we already don't got."

"When you rich," said Wise Pierre, "you can hire folks to not do work for you. Then you can not do twice as much as you ain't done before. That's rit-ma-tick."

"Marie-Louise, *très jolie*," said Foolish Pierre. "I'd like a very pretty wife, me."

"But she can't marry us all," said Big Pierre.

"That her problem," said Foolish Pierre. "Don't make me think about it. My brain starting to hurt."

"I hear that Swamp Ogre one mean critter," said Fat Pierre. "He eat up folks."

Wise Pierre said, "Four of us against one of him. We bound to win. That more rit-ma-tick."

They were making plans to set out the next morning, when Little Pierre returned from checking his muskrat traps. "Hello there," he said friendly-like. "What you so excited about?" Deep inside, he always hoped his brothers would someday decide they liked him.

But Big Pierre said, "Runt got big ears. Go on with you."

His brothers kept quiet until Little Pierre went to feed the chickens. But he knew they were up to something, so he decided to watch them closely. His brothers were lazybones, but they worked hard at being foolish. Little Pierre knew, sooner or later, he'd have to help them out of a big hole they'd dig for themselves.

The next morning Big Pierre, Fat Pierre, Wise Pierre,
and Foolish Pierre got up when the rooster crowed.
Little Pierre got up, too. "Where you headed to?" he asked.
But they just scooted him back into the cabin, and

off they went into the woods. Little Pierre filled
his pockets with buttons from their *maman*'s sewing
box, and followed. Always thinking, he dropped the
buttons to mark his path through the forest.

About evening, the older brothers reached a place where the trail branched out every which way. Something screeched in the woods, making them huddle together fearfully.

"That a *rou garou* for true," whispered Foolish Pierre, a little too loudly.

"That an owl, you fraidy cat," said Big Pierre.

"But it too late to find Marie-Louise. We better get home, us."

Just when they realized they were lost, Little Pierre appeared.

"You been following us?" asked Big Pierre very suspiciously.

"But of course," said the smallest brother. "I hear how you gonna rescue Marie-Louise. Me, I wanna help."

"Can't help," said Fat Pierre, "unless you know the way home."

"I can show you the path," said Little Pierre. "In return you gotta swear I can help you find Marie-Louise."

When his brothers refused, Little Pierre said, "You don't promise, you don't go home." They grumbled, but they agreed. So Little Pierre led them back, following the button trail.

The next morning Big Pierre, Fat Pierre, Wise Pierre, and Foolish Pierre decided to leave Little Pierre behind again, never mind their promise. They set out before the rooster crowed, carrying bread to leave a trail of crumbs. Fat Pierre said, "Bread better than buttons because we can eat what left over."

When Little Pierre found his brothers gone, he followed, laughing because they didn't have sense enough to know that the bread trail to lead them home would also lead Little Pierre to them.

Before long he overtook them. "Found you all!" he teased.

"How you do that?" asked a puzzled Big Pierre.

"I got my ways," Little Pierre said. His brothers looked at each other and tried to guess. But Foolish Pierre complained, "All this thinking make my head hurt." So they stopped thinking and let their brother come along.

At dusk Big Pierre said, "It too late. Can't find Marie-Louise in the dark. We better get home."

But they found that birds had eaten the bread crumbs.

"Now what we gonna do?" wailed Foolish Pierre. "Big old *rou garou* gonna get us for sure."

"Best we climb up some oak tree for the night," said Little Pierre. "At sunup we can keep looking for Marie-Louise."

"Hey!" said Fat Pierre suddenly. "I see lights in the distance. Whoever live there mebbe give us a big-big supper."

Even Little Pierre agreed to seek shelter for the night. To their astonishment the door to the big cabin was opened by Marie-Louise, the rich man's daughter, who was holding a broom.

"How you doing, Miss Marie-Louise?" said Big Pierre to the lovely young woman. "What is this place?"

"This the home of the Swamp Ogre," she said. "He make me clean his cabin and cook his supper."

"You can put down that broom," said Big Pierre. "We here to rescue you. All except Little Pierre. He just a tagalong."

"Where that Swamp Ogre?" asked Little Pierre.

"He in the woods," said Marie-Louise, "but he back soon."

Just then, through the trees, came the big old Swamp Ogre.

"Poo-yi!" said Little Pierre. "He smell as bad as he look, him."

"Tell me again that rit-ma-tick about how four o' us—mebbe five, countin' Little Pierre—gonna win if we fight one ogre," Big Pierre hissed to Wise Pierre.

"This ogre big as *ten* men," his brother said quickly. "His rit-ma-tick better than mine, 'cause ten always beat five."

"What we got here?" growled the Swamp Ogre.

"Just some lost folks," said quick-thinking Marie-Louise.

"We wondering could we stay till sunup?" Little Pierre asked, leading his brothers to play along.

"Sure thing," agreed the ogre. But Little Pierre spied the evil grin the monster tried to hide behind his upraised claw. While Marie-Louise cooked a mess of gumbo, she warned Little Pierre, "Watch out. That Swamp Ogre tricksy. He kill and eat you as soon as look at you."

After supper, as usual, the ogre locked Marie-Louise in a cupboard, placing the key on the ledge above the door. Then he sent the brothers to bed in the attic. There the Pierres found five beds, with a white-white nightcap on each. The older brothers eagerly put these on, climbed into bed, and fell asleep, snoring loudly.

But Little Pierre lifted the attic trapdoor and saw the ogre pick up his club and wait, listening. Little Pierre, being so smart, could see the monster wanted to make sure everyone was asleep. Then he would climb up and finish off the brothers.

Quickly Little Pierre made a plan, then called down, "I can't sleep without a drink of water."

"I get some," grumbled the ogre. He left the cabin; then Little Pierre heard him lower a bucket into the well. The boy woke his brothers, and told them to roll up the bedclothes and top them with the nightcaps. Then he had the brothers hide under the beds.

When the Swamp Ogre returned with a bucket of water, Little Pierre scrambled down the ladder, drank some, thanked the ogre politely, and climbed back to hide under his own bed.

A short time later, up came the ogre. Pierre saw him grin at the row of white nightcaps shining in the dark, raise his club, and— *boom! whack! crash! whump! thump!*—smack each white cap, then pound up and down along the rolled-up bedding that he mistook for the brothers. Little Pierre heard him singing as he worked:

"*Fat and thin* (WHACK!), *big and small* (CRACK!),
My club tenderize you all (CRACK-SMACK!).
And tomorrow (BUMP!), *I tell you* (THUMP!),
You'll be a tasty stew (THUMP-WHUMP!).*"

He gave an extra *thwack!* to the blanket he thought was Little Pierre, muttering, "That for makin' me fetch water!" Then, chuckling, he climbed down the ladder. Soon Little Pierre saw him curl up in a big chair by the fire and fall asleep.

Little Pierre signaled his brothers to follow quietly. Nearly paralyzed with fear, they tiptoed after him around the sleeping monster. Little Pierre took the key from the ledge and unlocked the cupboard door for Marie-Louise. Then they all hurried into the woods.

Near dawn they heard a terrible bellow far behind.
"That Swamp Ogre find we get away!" cried Little Pierre.
"Everybody move quick-quick." But the path ran alongside
a stream, and they began to sink in mud.

Suddenly a horrible head rose from
the water, followed by the long body of a
twelve-legged alligator. The gator eyed
the brothers and Marie-Louise
hungrily. "Whoee! I'm eatin'
mighty fine this mornin'!"
he growled happily.

"Best start with me,"
said Little Pierre. "I so
tired runnin', being
ate don't seem half
bad. But I'd 'preciate
you tellin' me one
thing, Mr. Gator."

"I ain't in the habit of talkin' with my vittles," said the gator. "But you bein' so agreeable, what you wanna know?"

"How you work all them legs?" asked Little Pierre.

"I ain't studied that before," said the gator, sounding uncertain. "It just *happen*."

"Nothin' just happen," Little Pierre said. "Me, I guess that leg go first, then that, then that one, then that one there. Next—let me see—*that* one." Each time the boy pointed to a different leg. Then he said, "What you think, Marie-Louise?"

The clever girl said, "You wrong! I say he move that one first, then that one, then this, then that one."

Big Pierre, Fat Pierre, Wise Pierre, and Foolish Pierre got into the game. They all began to point and shout, "This leg! That leg! This! That! This! That!"

Little Pierre turned to the gator. "Well, how *is* it you run?"

The gator was confused. "Why, er, this one—that is, I think it this one go first. No, that can't be! Must be that one back there move first. Yes. NO! That wrong, too. Mebbe these front ones move, then these. No, that's not working, neither!"

While he was studying, Little Pierre yelled, "Run!"

"Wait!" the gator bellowed. He tried to run, but he tangled up all his legs and lay flopping in the mud.

Now the noise of the Swamp Ogre was louder than ever.

Ahead, where the stream widened into a river, what looked like a big yellow bridge stretched from side to side.

Little Pierre saw two huge eyes pop open, and a mouth like a cave yawn in front of him. It was the biggest mud catfish he had ever seen.

"I been waiting for something tasty," said the catfish. He opened his mouth wider. "Hop in."

Little Pierre ran back to the others. They heard the Swamp Ogre pushing through trees no more than twenty paces back. Quickly Little Pierre arranged them in a line, himself—the smallest—in front, Big Pierre—the tallest—at the back. He told them, "You follow me, one at a time, and say, 'Let me cross, Mr. Catfish, and eat my bigger brother behind me.' "

Then Little Pierre ran up, shouting, "Mr. Catfish, let me cross, and you can have my big sister right behind me."

"Go on," said the fish. Up and over went Little Pierre.

Next came Marie-Louise, who shouted, "Let me cross, Mr. Catfish, and eat my bigger brother behind me."

In this way, Marie-Louise, Fat Pierre, Wise Pierre, and Foolish Pierre got safely across. At last Big Pierre cried, "Hey, Mr. Catfish, let me cross, and you can have my bigger brother right behind me. He's the tastiest one of all."

As Big Pierre jumped off the catfish's tail,
Little Pierre saw the Swamp Ogre ready to
climb the slimy, scaly bridge.

"You got a bigger brother?" asked the catfish.

"Ain't no one bigger 'n me, you overgrowed minnow!"
said the ogre. "Now let me cross and catch my runaway
stew meat!"

"Poo-yi! He sure smell bad," said the catfish, who
swallowed the ogre in one gulp, "but he don't taste half
bad, him." Then he sank contentedly into the river.

When they got home, Marie-Louise naturally
decided to marry Little Pierre. And her *papa*
gave him a reward. So they got themselves a
farm and worked to make a success of it. Without
their brother to do all the work, Big Pierre, Fat Pierre,
Wise Pierre, and Foolish Pierre had to help their
papa and *maman*. But the four of them didn't
equal the worth of their littlest brother.

That's rit-ma-tick. And that's all.

Author's Note

The adventures of Little Pierre are based on the stories of Poucet or Ti-Poucet (Little Tom Thumb; Thumbling), well known to French-tradition storytellers in the New World. I have consulted variants from a variety of sources. Among the most useful were Barry Jean Ancelet, *Cajun and Creole Folktales: The French Oral Tradition of South Louisiana* (New York: Garland Publishing, 1994); Alcée Fortier, *Louisiana Folk-Tales: In French Dialect and English Translation*, Memoirs of the American Folk-Lore Society, vol. 2 (1895; reprint, New York: Kraus Reprint Co., 1969); Ray Robinson, *Cajun Tales of the Louisiana Bayous* (Gray, LA: Cypress Publishers, 1984); and Corinne L. Saucier, trans., *Folk Tales from French Louisiana* (New York: Exposition Press, 1962; reprint, Baton Rouge, LA: Claitor's Publishing Division, 1972). Other helpful volumes include Carl Lindahl, Maida Owens, and C. Renee Harvison, eds., *Swapping Stories: Folktales from Louisiana* (Jackson: University Press of Mississippi, 1997); Rosemary Hyde Thomas, trans., *It's Good to Tell You: French Folktales from Missouri* (Colombia: University of Missouri Press, 1981); Richard M. Dorson, *Buying the Wind: Regional Folklore in the United States* (Chicago: University of Chicago Press, 1964); and J. J. Reneaux, *Haunted Bayou: And Other Cajun Ghost Stories* (Little Rock, AR: August House, 1994), as well as her *Cajun Folktales* (Little Rock, AR: August House, 1992), also available on audiocassette. A variety of collateral readings provided information on Cajun life and lore. A number of variants of the Ti-Poucet stories can also be found in Elsie Clews Parsons, *Folk-Lore of the Antilles, French and English*, Memoirs of the American Folk-Lore Society, vol. 26, (New York: 1943). Many of the incidents described are recognizable as parallels of European Tom Thumb tales.